T0353812

POISON RIVER

MODESTO MCCLEAN

AuthorHouse™
1663 Liberty Drive
Bloomington, IN 47403
www.authorhouse.com
Phone: 833-262-8899

Because of the dynamic nature of the Internet, any web addresses or links contained in this book may have changed since publication and may no longer be valid. The views expressed in this work are solely those of the author and do not necessarily reflect the views of the publisher, and the publisher hereby disclaims any responsibility for them.

Any people depicted in stock imagery provided by Getty Images are models, and such images are being used for illustrative purposes only.
Certain stock imagery © Getty Images.

This book is printed on acid-free paper.

ISBN: 979-8-8230-0973-7 (sc)
      979-8-8230-0974-4 (hc)
      979-8-8230-0975-1 (e)

Library of Congress Control Number: 2023911214

Print information available on the last page.

Published by AuthorHouse 06/16/2023

authorHOUSE®

8

9

11

12

Dr. Asad: Good evening everyone, my name is Asad. My fellow colleagues and students have been working on idea for how to remove Sarin from the river. Let me explain this in the scale model that we built. Here are some facts on situation:

1. We cannot stop the river but we can slow it down at several dams, giving us time to remove the Sarin before it flows downstream
2. Since Sarin is colorless we must first mark it with a stain to visually track it
3. We found yellow dye called flourecein sticks to Sarin
4. The dams should be shut down temporarily stopping the flow of the water
5. Next, the contaminated water must be treated before over flowing downstream
6. Treatment will consist of separating the Sarin from the river water. We found Sarin has a greater affinity to paper type filters than water
7. Once trapped in filters, they need to be incinerated

General Franks: Dr. Asad you are a genius

14

15

16

19

24

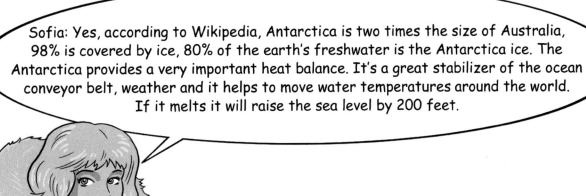

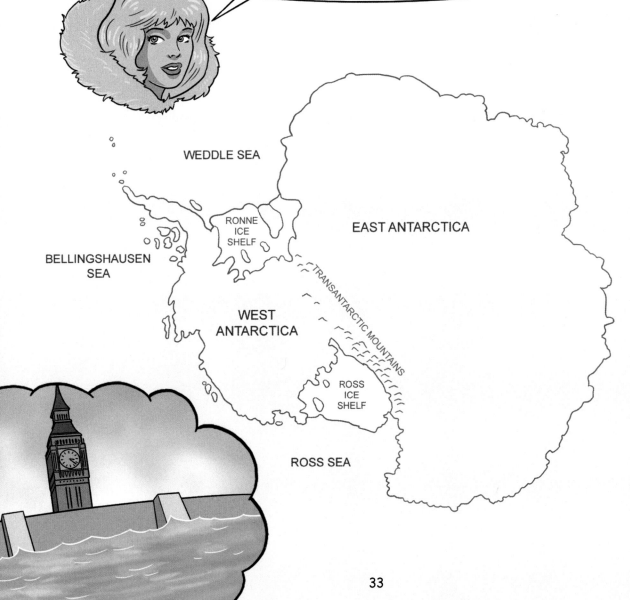

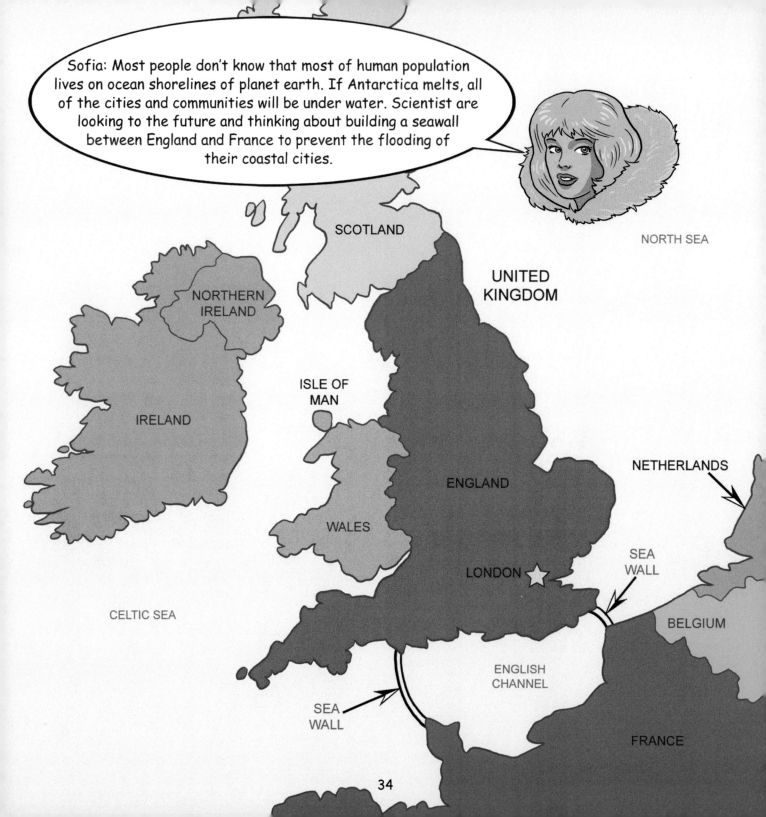

38

42

43

44

47

51

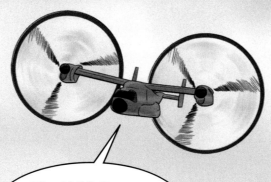

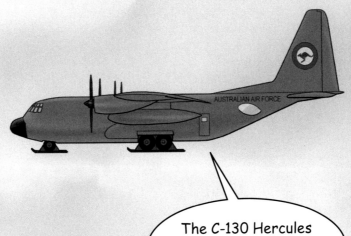

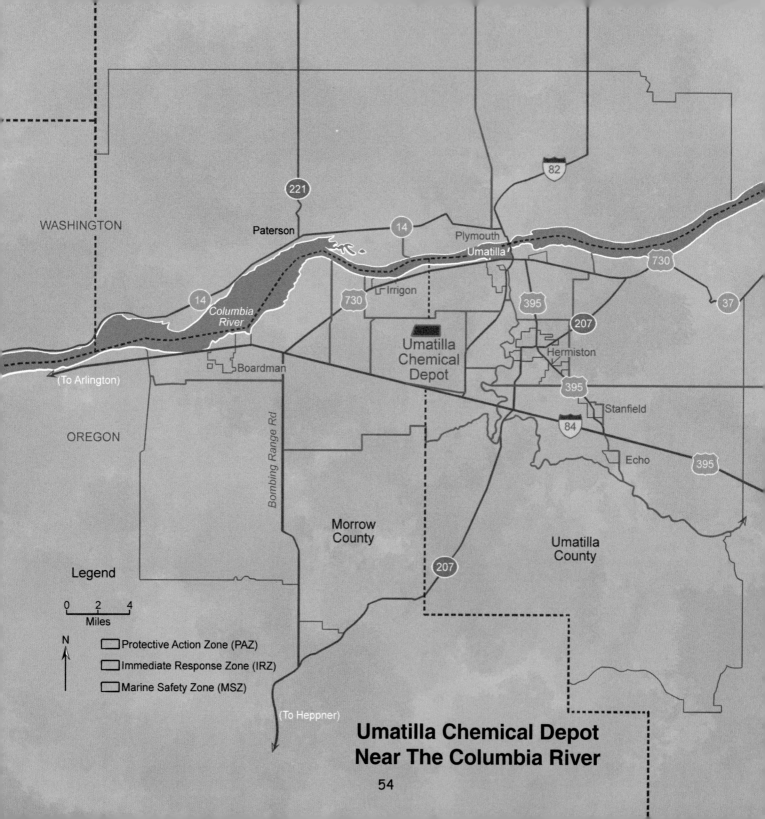

**Umatilla Chemical Depot
Near The Columbia River**

54

Canada Geese are the largest geese in the world, weight range is 5-20lbs and can fly day or night due to their incredible stamina. They migrate from Northern Canada to Northern Mexico using earth's magnetic field for direction. When migrating they use flyways or routes called Pacific, Central and Mississippi Flyways. They are herbivores, and generally mate for life.

Fascinating Animal Facts

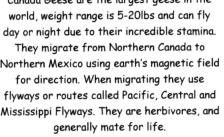

Penguin are aquatic flightless birds mostly living in the Southern Hemisphere including the South Pole. They are carnivorous and eat krill, squid and fish, and the wings have adapted to become flippers propelling them underwater for many minutes at a time. They also tend to have the same mate for life. Huddling is an important survival technique with the birds bunching together during cold weather to conserve heat.

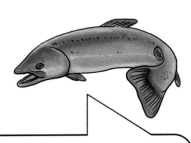

Salmon hatch in fresh water, migrate to ocean water, and come back to spawn in fresh water. They use the earth's magnetic compass and sense of smell to return to their birthplace to spawn. Most species of salmon die after spawning. They are commonly found in the Pacific and Atlantic waters. Most all fish from the ocean canot survive in fresh water and most all fresh water fish canot survive in the ocean. Salmon can live both waters.

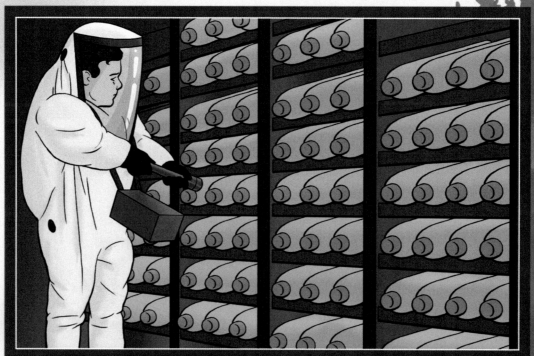

**Chemical Bunker Housing
Chemical and Biological Weapons**

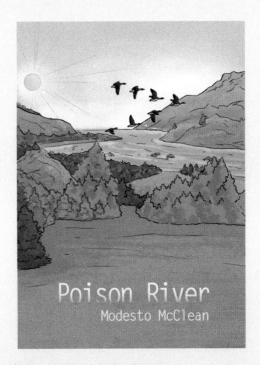

More Adventures of Dr. O'Hara Coming Soon.

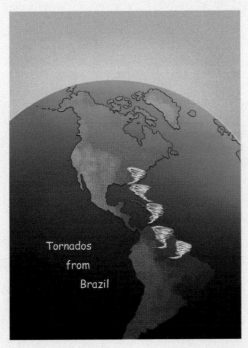

Tornados
from
Brazil

Please join Dr. O'Hara in his next adventure,
"Tornadoes From Brazil"

On July 20, 1969 I was one of millions of people all over the world that saw Neil Armstrong walk on the moon. For many years to follow there was the cliché, "if we can go to the moon, we can do anything". I hope my books inspire the next generation of pioneers "that candoanything" including solving and, better yet, prevention of environmental disasters.

What's that JR?, end with an animal joke? Why did the bubble gum cross the road? Because it was stuck on the bottom of the chicken's foot...haha..

Printed in the United States
by Baker & Taylor Publisher Services